LEBANON

COUNTRIES IN CRISIS

Rourke Publishing

www.rourkepublishing.com

PHOTO CREDITS: Alinari/Topfoto: pp. 32-33; Archivo Iconografico, S. A./Corbis: p. 13; Maher
Attar/Sygma/Corbis: pp. 30, 39; Joseph Barrack/AFP/Getty Images: p. 37; Bettmann/Corbis: pp. 20-21, 25;
Frank and Frances Carpenter Collection/Library of Congress: p. 17; Corbis: p. 42; Robert J. Fluegel. U. S.
Navy/Department of Defense: p. 5; Bill Foley/Time & Life Pictures/Getty Images: p. 14; David
Freund/istockphoto.com: p. 22; Ancho Gosh/Gini/Corbis: p. 6; Ramzi Haidar/AFP/Getty Images: p. 35;
PHC Chet King/Department of Defense: p. 28; Library of Congress: pp. 9, 10, 16; Nabil Mounzer/EPA/Corbis:
p. 7; Marwan Naamani/AFP/Getty Images: p. 34; Michael Palis/istockphoto.com: p. 15; Scott Peterson/Getty
Images: p. 38; Gerard Rancinan/Sygma/Corbis: pp. 26-27; Topham Picturepoint: p. 19; Dennis
Whitehead/Corbis: p. 29.

Cover picture shows Lebanese citizens on a scooter in a part of Beirut. This region was hit by Israeli attacks during
the summer of 2006 [Burak Kara/Vatan Daily/Getty Images].

Produced for Rourke Publishing by Discovery Books
Editors: Amy Bauman, Gill Humphrey
Designer: Keith Williams
Map: Stefan Chabluk
Photo researcher: Rachel Tisdale

Library of Congress Cataloging-in-Publication Data

Stewart, James, 1950-
  Lebanon / James Stewart.
      p. cm. -- (Countries in crisis)
  ISBN 978-1-60044-617-7
  1. Lebanon--History--Juvenile literature. I. Title.
  DS80.9.S74 2008
  956.92--dc22

                                    2007020676

Printed in the USA

CONTENTS

CHAPTER ONE

THE BATTLEGROUND

In July and August 2006, the people of Lebanon got caught in a war. It was a war most of them did not want. Some 1,200 people were killed. Thousands were hurt and over 250,000 people fled their homes.

Day after day, the Lebanese stayed in their basements. Outside, jet airplanes bombed roads, bridges, and power plants. Big guns pounded towns and villages. Tanks rolled across the border. Ships along the coast rained shells onto the land.

The war ended on August 14. By then, 400 miles (640 kilometers) of road had been wrecked. Also 2 hospitals, 350 schools, 25 gas stations, and 15,000 homes had been flattened. Another 130,000

homes had been damaged. Lebanon was a country in crisis.

ISRAEL

Lebanon's attacker was its small but powerful neighbor, Israel. What made this country act so violently?

Before Israel was created many Jewish people lived in an area known as Palestine. They wanted a country of their own. Other Western countries agreed and, in 1948, Israel was formed from land still occupied by many Palestinians. Israel is surrounded by Arab countries—Lebanon, Syria, Jordan, and Egypt. They attacked Israel at once. They wanted to destroy the new country. They failed, as they did in several later wars. The

A city under fire. Israeli bombs strike Beirut, the capital of Lebanon, during the war of summer 2006.

An Israeli gun fires into southern Lebanon. War broke out after Lebanese guerrillas had captured two Israeli soldiers.

losers, however, were the Palestinian Arabs. Since Israel was created, many have fled. Others live as second-class citizens within Israel.

HEZBOLLAH

In 1982, a group of Palestinians and their **Muslim** supporters formed an organization called Hezbollah. This name means the "Party of God." The group's goal was to destroy Israel. Over the years, Hezbollah has become very powerful in Lebanon. In 2006, it had 23 seats in the **National Assembly**.

On July 12, 2006, Hezbollah **guerrillas** went into Israel. They attacked an army patrol and captured two soldiers. In response, Israel attacked Lebanon. The war was terrible. But it is only one of many sad events that has hurt Lebanon.

A TERRIBLE SITUATION

" The situation here is terrible. . .because of the war. Everybody is hoping for peace, but Israel and America are determined to get rid of Hezbollah— which is just fighting to defend Lebanon's rights. . . .

Ahmed Taher, a Palestinian refugee in Lebanon

"

Sheik Hassan Nasrallah claims victory over Israel, September 2006. The sheik was the leader of Hezbollah, an anti-Israeli group based in Lebanon. He claimed victory because his forces had not been defeated.

CHAPTER TWO

ANCIENT ANCESTORS

Lebanon is a small country that sits at the eastern end of the Mediterranean Sea, between Israel and Syria. About 3.8 million people live there. Its geography is varied. The 135-mile (216-kilometer) coast is full of beaches and rocky bays. Inland are the Lebanon Mountains. Their snow-capped peaks rise to 10,000 feet (3,000 meters). Then the land drops into the rich Beqaa and Litani valleys.

WHERE IS LEBANON?

LEBANON is in the Middle East

Tripoli

Asi River

BEIRUT

Litani River

Mediterranean Sea

Sidon

SYRIA

Damascus

Tyre

ISRAEL

km
0   30
0   30
miles

The beauty of Lebanon is seen between the country's famous cedar trees. Behind, Mount Lebanon soars into the clear sky.

To the East are more mountains. The Litani River flows between the two mountain ranges. It runs into the sea near the city of Tyre. This large river is the only one that flows all year round.

The country's summers are long, hot, and dry. Winter brings rain and, away from the coast, the temperatures can drop below freezing.

PHOENICIA

Lebanon has a long, interesting history. Over the years, it has attracted settlers from many different racial and religious groups.

CHANGING NAMES

The name Lebanon comes from the word Laban. This was the ancient name for the area. In early times, it was usually called "Phoenicia" after the Phoenician people. After the Roman conquest the area was simply part of Syria. Lebanon did not reemerge as a separate country until the twentieth century.

The temples at Baalbek, Lebanon, were once the mightiest in the Roman world. Today, although in ruins, they are still magnificent.

THE AGE OF TYRE

> I made a voyage to Tyre in Phoenicia, because I had heard that there was a temple there. . . . I asked how long ago the temple had been built, and . . .they said that the temple was as ancient as Tyre itself, and that Tyre had already stood for two thousand three hundred years.

The Greek historian Herodotus (484–425 B.C.)

By about 2500 B.C. the area of present-day Lebanon was called Phoenicia. The Phoenicians were famous for their trading and sailing skills. They had strong ties to ancient Egypt and **colonies** as far away as North Africa and Spain. The Lebanese cities of Tyre and Sidon were built at this time.

By the end of the ninth century B.C., other groups of people wanted to control the trade routes that the Phoenicians had built. Phoenicia was conquered many times. First, it was the Assyrians, and then the Babylonians. In 332 B.C., the Greek army of Alexander the Great took control of the region. The Romans arrived around 270 years later and made Phoenicia part of their empire. Under Roman rule, Beirut grew into a large city and Christianity was introduced.

DRUZE

The Druze religion grew out of Islam. This was in the tenth and eleventh centuries. Its followers do not think of themselves as Muslims. The faith is said to be named after the supposed founder, Muhammad ad-Darazi. Lebanon is the religion's homeland, although followers are found all around the world. During the Lebanese **Civil War** (1975-1990), the Druze and the Christians fought each other.

Phoenicia remained part of the Roman Empire until the seventh century A.D. when the Arabs conquered the area. They brought the religion of Islam and the Arabic language to the region.

RELIGIOUS DIFFERENCES

Between the eleventh and thirteenth centuries, Christian soldiers came from Western Europe. These were the crusaders. They wanted to conquer the **Holy Land**. This included the seaports of modern Lebanon. By the time the **crusades** ended, the area was home to people of many different religions.

Christians had been in the region since Roman times. Many of them belonged to the **Maronite** church. Some were also Roman Catholics. Later, Protestants began living there.

Muslim followers belonged mainly to two groups, or sects. These are the Shia and the Sunni. Members of the Shia sect settled in the north. The Sunni became the

Christian soldiers fight Muslims during the Fifth Crusade (1219). Even today, many Muslims blame Christians for attacking their lands all those years ago.

SHIA AND SUNNI

Islam has two main sects. These are the Shi'a and Sunni. This split occurred after the death of Islam's founder, the Prophet Muhammad. The two groups could not agree on who best should lead the faith. Shia believe the true leaders of Islam are the descendants of the Prophet Muhammad. The Sunni believe the leaders should be people descended from Muhammad's companions. Disagreement between the two groups has sometimes led to violence.

Lebanon is a country with many faiths. A Maronite Christian priest says a prayer. The service was for the victims of a car bomb.

TOURIST'S DREAM

In times of peace, Lebanon is a great place to visit. People come from all over the world to see its ruins. These include Byblos, one of the oldest inhabited cities in the world. Tyre and Baalbek are sites of Roman ruins. Anjar is the site of an early Islamic city. Qadisha is the site of a cedar forest and ancient Christian holy places.

Byblos Castle, Lebanon. Christian crusaders built this fortress in the eleventh century. They used stones taken from the remains of Roman buildings.

majority in the south. A third group was the Druze.

All of these religions existed in one small region. Understanding and tolerance were important if these religions were to exist peacefully side by side. Sadly, once modern Lebanon was created, this did not always happen.

CHAPTER THREE

BALANCING ACT

At last, the crusaders were driven from the **Middle East**. Then, the region that is modern Lebanon became part of the Egyptian Mamluk Empire. This lasted until 1516 when the Ottoman Turks came from the north. They conquered the area and divided it. Some regions were governed locally, while others were governed from the Ottoman capital, Constantinople. Under Ottoman

A flourishing port. This photo shows Beirut in the late nineteenth century. Then, Lebanon was still part of the Turkish Ottoman Empire.

AMERICAN UNIVERSITY OF BEIRUT

The American University of Beirut opened in 1866. Then it was called the Syrian Protestant College. The school had sixteen students when it began. From the start, men of any color, race, or religion could attend. Today, the school has 6,900 students and is open to both men and women.

The American University of Beirut in the 1920s. It was set up by Protestant Christians. The university did much to help Lebanon move into the modern world.

rule, the Lebanese found some peace. Beirut became a major port. As the region prospered so the population grew, too.

But in the 1800s, Lebanon's religious groups began fighting. Following a massacre of Maronites by the Druze, in 1860, the French

SHARED POWER

Lebanon has worked to keep peace between its religious groups. Since 1926, each of the country's main leadership positions have been held by people from different religious groups. In the past, the president has been a Maronite Christian. The prime minister was a Sunni Muslim and the speaker of the National Assembly was a Shia Muslim. This plan was meant to keep any group from having too much power.

led a force to restore order there. In 1881, French **Jesuits** set up the Roman Catholic Université Saint-Joseph in Beirut. There was also a Protestant college opened by American **missionaries** in 1866.

Under Western protection, Lebanon's Christians did well. They became better educated and wealthier than the Muslim working class. This growing difference between the two groups was the cause of many of Lebanon's future troubles.

INDEPENDENCE

During World War I, the Ottomans sided with Germany and its **allies**. This led to Germany's enemies occupying Lebanon. By 1918, the country was under French military occupation. The modern state of Greater Lebanon was established in 1920 and the French were given the job of preparing

Beirut, where East meets West. This photo of a 1950s Beirut street scene could be anywhere in the United States or Europe at that time.

it for independence. The trouble was not all Lebanese wanted independence. Some wanted Lebanon to unite with Syria to become part of a larger Arab state.

Lebanon flourished between the World Wars. All the while, it carefully balanced the interests of its people's different religions. It was occupied again during

World War II, but by 1946, the French finally withdrew. Lebanon was now a fully independent country. It became a member of both the **United Nations (UN)** and the **Arab League**.

For 25 years after independence, Lebanon survived as a **democracy**. But, the system came under strain. First, there was the problem of the largely Christian middle class. Although they were now out-numbered by Muslims, they had more than an equal share of the country's wealth. Second, by the mid-1950s, **Arab nationalism** was sweeping the Middle East. This movement called all Arabs to unite against the Western powers that

Riots in Beirut, 1958. U.S. Marines helped restore law and order, but Lebanon's problems were not solved.

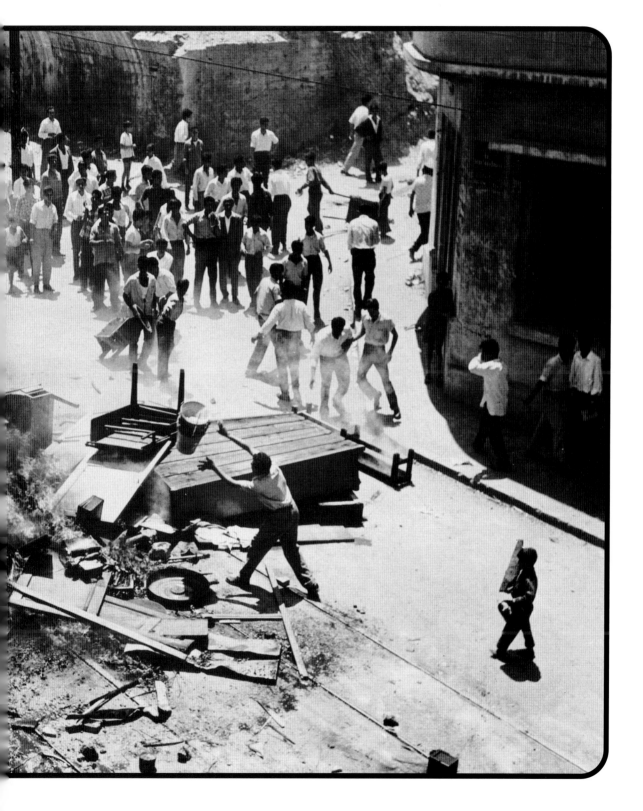

THE LEBANESE TABLE

Lebanon is famous for its food. This country is the place where French and Middle Eastern food comes together. Its tasty dishes are found nowhere else in the world. Lebanese wine from the Beqaa Valley has been produced since Roman times. It is specially made to go with the local food.

Lebanese cooking mixes together the finest recipes from the Middle East, Turkey, and France.

had controlled the region for the first half of the century.

Two other factors made the situation more tricky. One was the appearance of Israel on Lebanon's southern border. This led to the arrival of large numbers of Muslim Palestinian refugees in 1948. The other factor was Syria. This unstable country had been linked to Lebanon in the past, and it wanted to see the two countries united again.

The first serious threat to the young country's peace came in 1949. A Syrian-backed attempt to overthrow the Lebanese government failed. Nine years later, the country was shaken again. This time by a large-scale revolt led by the mainly Muslim working class.

The president at the time, Camille Chamoun, could not ask the army to restore order. He feared that its Muslim troops would not act against fellow Muslims. Instead, Chamoun turned to the United Nations for help. The United Nations sent U.S. troops, and gradually order was restored. However, nothing had been resolved and worse was yet to come.

CHAPTER FOUR

YEARS OF WAR

Lebanon settled down after the crisis of 1958. Fuad Chehab was president from 1958 to 1964. Charles Hélou was president from 1964 to 1970. Both presidents encouraged the country's growth and tried to help the downtrodden Muslims.

But Lebanon was changing. Two-thirds of the population now lived in Beirut. The city was divided along the same religious lines as the rest of the country. However, most of the poorer Muslims still worked in the countryside. The Muslims had another complaint. In 1967 and 1973, other Arab countries had gone to war with Israel, but Lebanon had remained **neutral**. Why, the Muslims asked, had the country not gone to the aid of their fellow Arabs?

THE HAPPIEST PERIOD

Between 1943 and 1970, Lebanon had its happiest period. We were free and independent.

Pierre Gemayel, a Maronite Christian, 1985

This photograph clearly shows one of Lebanon's major problems. The city in the background is wealthy, but people living in the nearby refugee camp have almost nothing.

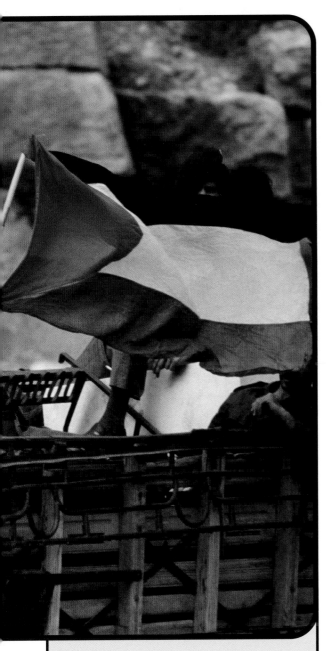

After 1970, large numbers of Palestinian fighters, members of the PLO, made their base in Lebanon. This caused huge problems for the country.

Finally, there were the Palestinians. In 1948, some 100,000 Palestinian refugees flooded into Lebanon from Israel. Another 170,000 came in 1967. These people were homeless and poor. In Lebanon, they lived in crowded and unhealthy refugee camps. After 1967, members of a group called the Palestinian Liberation Organization (PLO) began living in the camps, too. They used both the camps and the nearby areas as bases. From there, they attacked Israel. In 1970, the situation became more dangerous. As the PLO was driven from Jordan another four thousand of their fighters came to Lebanon. Many Lebanese, especially the Christians, did not want the PLO in their country.

Children play while the U.S. Army prepares to pull out, 1984. American forces were sent to Lebanon to try to bring peace. They were not very successful.

WAR

By the early 1970s, Palestinians were clashing with the Lebanese Army and the Israeli Defense Force (IDF). Civil war broke out in 1975. It lasted until 1990. Many different forces and conflicts were involved. These included:

- Christian **militias**, led by a group called the Phalange
- Shi'a and Sunni Muslim militias
- Palestinian militias, mainly the PLO and, after 1982, Hezbollah
- Israel Defense Forces
- The Syrian Army
- Peacekeeping forces from the United Nations, the United States, and other countries

PLO

The Palestinian Liberation Organization (PLO) began in 1964. Yasser Arafat led the group. Its goal was to give Palestine back to the Palestinian Arabs. The PLO was not powerful. It could not fight Israel head on. So it used **terrorist** tactics. Many people do not agree with this kind of fighting, and because of this the PLO lost support across the world.

Yasser Arafat attends a conference in Beirut in 1981.

29

SYRIAN POINT OF VIEW

> In 1975, civil war broke out in Lebanon. In 1976, Syrian troops [went into] Lebanon upon request from the Lebanese President. The troops in Lebanon [faced the] Israeli army in 1982. . . .In 1990, Syria and its allies in Lebanon [put] an end to the fifteen-year-old civil war and Syrian troops remained in Lebanon to [keep peace] and stability.

The Syrian government explains why its soldiers were in Lebanon

A heavily-armed Syrian soldier on duty in Lebanon, 1990. The Syrian Army had helped bring Lebanon's civil war to an end.

The civil war was one of the worst in recent history. Lebanon was torn to pieces. Over 100,000 Lebanese and 20,000 Palestinians died. In the confusion, Muslim killed Muslim, and Christian killed Christian. The IDF backed the Christians. At first, the Syrians attacked them. Later, they switched sides because Syria feared that a Muslim victory would provoke an Israeli invasion of its country.

The fighting turned Beirut into a ghost town. Across the country, roads, houses, schools, hospitals, bridges, and power plants were destroyed. Hundreds of thousands of Lebanese fled the country.

REASONS FOR ATTACK

" We could have gone on seeing our civilians injured. . . .We could have gone on counting those killed by explosive charges left in a Jerusalem supermarket or. . .bus stop. All the orders to carry out these acts. . .came from Beirut [the PLO]. Should we have reconciled ourselves to the ceaseless killing of civilians. . . ?

Israeli Prime Minister Menachem Begin tells why Israeli forces moved into Lebanon in 1982

"

The price of war as seen in the ruins of Beirut. The civil war lasted on and off for more than ten years.

PEACE OF A SORT

Eventually, the Israelis withdrew to the south. The Syrian army got the different Lebanese groups to stop killing each other and so the war ended. **Hostages** that were taken during the war were released. The Lebanese government began peace talks with Israel. Rafik Hariri, the new prime minister, began the job of repairing and rebuilding the country. **Mines** were cleared. Communications were re-established. Beirut began to look like a normal city again.

But not everything went easily. Hezbollah did not want people to forget the Palestinians. It continued fighting with Israel as it had since the 1980s. The IDF responded with force. Lebanon's future was still far from bright.

CHAPTER FIVE

CRISIS RETURNS

Life must go on. Lebanese farmers ready their land for planting, but they risk being killed by unexploded bombs, March 2007.

Lebanon's land is not rich. The soil is mostly poor. Grain grows well only in the Beqaa Valley. Farmers make a modest living from crops such as fruit, tobacco, olives, and vegetables. Some also keep chickens, goats, sheep, and a few cows. The country has no oil. It has only a few valuable minerals. These include iron ore, building stone, and sand for glassmaking.

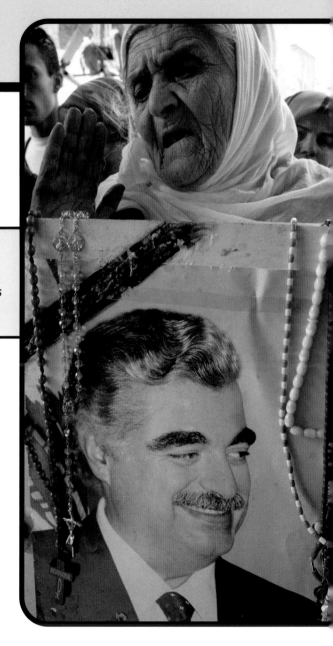

A Muslim woman holds a picture of Rafik Hariri. Muslims and Christians mourned together after a car bomb killed Lebanon's famous prime minister.

But before the war, Lebanon had become successful. It was one of the most prosperous countries of the region. The country owed its success to its people. The Lebanese were known for buying and selling, lending and borrowing, importing and exporting. But all of the things the Lebanese did so well depended on tolerance and peace. These disappeared during the civil war. Once they were gone, Lebanon crumbled.

HARIRI AND SYRIA

Rafik Hariri was a Sunni Muslim billionaire. He was also Lebanon's prime minister from

1992–1998 and from 2000–2004. While in office, he did much to rebuild Lebanon after the civil war. He even spent his own money on projects such as cleaning up Beirut and funding students' education.

During this time, Lebanon was still occupied. Syrian troops had been in the country since 1976. At first, Hariri accepted this. The army helped keep the peace.

But when Israel withdrew in 2000, Hariri decided that the Syrians were no longer needed. The United Nations agreed. They told the Syrian army to leave. Five years later, in February 2005, Rafik Hariri died in a car bombing. Many people blamed Syria for the **assassination** and demanded that Syrian troops leave the country. Syria's troops withdrew and its 30-year hold on Lebanon ended.

HEZBOLLAH

Hezbollah, the Party of God, is a radical Shia Muslim group. It was founded in 1982 to drive the Israelis from Lebanon. More recently, the organization has become a political party too. It has gained respect for its work with the country's poor. In 2004, the United Nations called for all Lebanese militias to disband. Hezbollah did not. It remains a powerful force along the southern Lebanon-Israel border.

Anti-Syrian protests in 2005. Many people blamed the Syrians for the killing of well-known Lebanese people like Rafik Hariri. They feared that Syria was trying to take over Lebanon.

HEZBOLLAH AND ISRAEL

In the south, the fighting between Israel and Hezbollah went on. Throughout the 1990s, Hezbollah

Supporters of Hezbollah clash with the army, 2007. They are calling for the Lebanese government to resign. Hezbollah wants Lebanon to be a more Muslim country.

often raided Israeli towns. Israel responded with air strikes. It also supported the largely Christian South Lebanese Army (SLA). This anti-Hezbollah militia was strong in the south.

When Israel withdrew its forces in 2000, the SLA collapsed. This gave Hezbollah control of southern Lebanon. From there, the group continued its raids until 2006 when the situation erupted into war.

These Palestinian refugee children were born in Lebanon. They have seen shooting and bombing all their lives.

LEBANON SPEAKS

> " My Fellow Lebanese. . .we find ourselves once again facing Israeli aggression [shown] in a continuous barrage of air, sea and land bombing which has spared no one. . . .This killing machine continues its devastation. . .with the single goal of inflicting as much pain as possible on the Lebanese people. "

Prime Minister Fuad Siniora speaks to the Lebanese people on July 15, 2006

Sadly, the conflict undid much of the reconstruction that had taken place since 1990. It also divided the Lebanese people. Some saw Hezbollah as freedom fighters and protectors. Others wished Hezbollah would let Lebanon return to its peaceful and tolerant way of life.

Meanwhile Syria was humiliated by its withdrawal in 2005. It still dreamed of a union with Lebanon. Israel had made it clear that it would continue to target anyone who threatened its security. Hundreds of thousands of Palestinian refugees still remained in Lebanon, backed by Hezbollah, but still without a country of their own. For its part, Hezbollah held on to its view that the state of Israel should not exist.

ISRAEL SPEAKS

> On July 12, 2006, Hezbollah carried out the most serious terrorist attack. . .since the IDF withdrew from Lebanon in May 2000. During the attack, 2 Israeli soldiers were abducted, 8 soldiers and 1 civilian woman were killed, and approximately 54 soldiers and civilians were wounded (as of noon on July 13). The Israeli government [holds]. . .the Lebanese government as solely responsible for the Hezbollah attack.
>
> *From the website of the Israeli state-sponsored Intelligence and Terrorism Information Center*

And behind all this lay the uneasy relations between Lebanon's many religious groups. Even by the middle of 2007, the future for Lebanon was very uncertain.

A BLEAK FUTURE

" It is hard to see a good future for Lebanon. The situation is very bad, we had to close our shop for weeks because of the conflict and now the local economy in Sidon is dead. We need cooperation between the different political sides in Lebanon so we can live in peace. "

Ali Dimashi, a Lebanese Sunni Muslim, speaking after the war

Danger for Lebanon's neighbors. An Israeli policeman examines the wreck of a car hit by a Hezbollah rocket. It had been fired from Lebanon.

TIMELINE

ca. 3000 The Phoenicians settle in
present-day Lebanon. During
ancient times the area is
called Phoenicia.

ca. 868 The Assyrians conquer Phoenicia.

ca. 600 The Babylonians conquer
Phoenicia.

ca. 538 The Persians conquer Phoenicia.

332 The Greeks take over control
of the region.

64 Phoenicia becomes part
of the Roman Empire.

A.D.

ca. 600 Maronites settle in the area.

630s The Arabs conquer the region.
They introduce the religion of
Islam and the Arabic language.

1114 The crusaders capture Tyre.

1280s The territory becomes part of
the Mamluk Egyptian Empire.

1517 The territory becomes part of
the Ottoman Empire.

1918 Allied forces occupy the region
at the end of World War I.

1920 Greater Lebanon is founded.

1923 France is given control
over Lebanon and Syria.

1943 Lebanon becomes independent.

1948 War with Israel and Palestinian
refugees arrive in the country.

1958 U.S. Marines sent to Lebanon
to restore order.

1967 More Palestinian refugees arrive

1975 The civil war begins.

1978 Israel invades Lebanon.

1982 The second Israeli invasion
reaches Beirut, PLO driven from
Lebanon, Hezbollah founded.

1990 The civil war ends.

1992 Rafik Hariri becomes
prime minister.

2005 Rafik Hariri is assassinated.

2006 Israeli land, sea, and air attacks
make up 34 days of war.

FACT FILE

LEBANON

GEOGRAPHY

Area: 4,015 square miles (10,400 sq km)

Borders: Israel, Syria

Terrain: Coastal plains, mountains, valleys

Highest point: Mount Qurnat as Sawda, 10,131 feet (3,088 m)

Resources: Stone, iron ore, fine sand

Major rivers: Litani

SOCIETY

Population: 3,870,000 plus 404,170 Palestinian refugees **Ethnic groups:** Arab 95% (although many Christians called themselves "Phoenician" rather than Arab); Armenian 4%; other 1%

Languages: Arabic; French; English; Armenian

Literacy: 93%

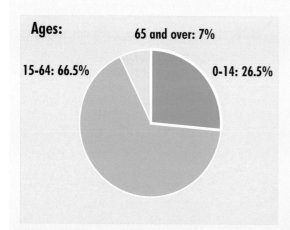

Ages:
- 65 and over: 7%
- 15-64: 66.5%
- 0-14: 26.5%

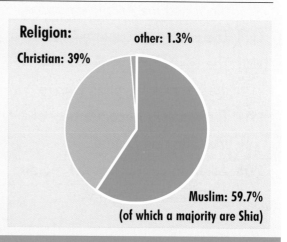

Religion:
- Christian: 39%
- other: 1.3%
- Muslim: 59.7% (of which a majority are Shia)

GOVERNMENT

Type: Democratic republic   **Capital**: Beirut   **Regions**: 8

Independence: November 22, 1943

Law: Mixture of Ottoman, religious, Napoleonic, and custom

Vote: All men over 21; only those women over 21 who have received an elementary education

System: President (chosen for 6 years), prime minister and cabinet, 128-seat National Assembly (elected every 4 years)

ECONOMY

Currency: Lebanese pound

Total value of goods and services (2005): $24 billion

Labor force (2001): 2.6 million Lebanese; 1 million foreigners

Poverty: 28% of the population below poverty line

Main industries (2005): Banking, tourism, food processing, jewelry, cement

Foreign debt (2005): $26 billion

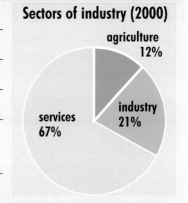

Sectors of industry (2000)

- agriculture 12%
- industry 21%
- services 67%

COMMUNICATIONS AND MEDIA

Telephones (2004): 630,000 fixed line; 888,000 mobile   **Internet users (2005):** 600,000

TV stations: 15 stations, including the Lebanese Broadcast Corporation

Newspapers: 7 main national papers, including An-Nahar (Arabic), L'Orient-Le Jour (French)

Radio: 4 main stations (e.g. state-run Radio Liban; Voice of Lebanon)

Airports: 7   **Railways:** 249 miles (401 km)   **Roads:** 4,536 miles (7,300 km)

Ships: 39 over 1,102 tons (1,000 tonnes)   **Ports:** Beirut, Chekka, Jounie, Tripoli

MILITARY

Branches: Army, navy, air force

Service: 12-month military service compulsory for all citizens over 18

GLOSSARY

allies (AL ize) — friendly countries that will support each other militarily

Arab League (A ruhb leeg) — an organization of Arab States. It was set up in 1945 to help support and protect the independence of the member countries.

Arab nationalism (A ruhb NASH uh nuh liz uhm) — a movement that encouraged Arab people to think of themselves as belonging to one nation. It began in the nineteenth century.

assassination (uh SASS un NAY shuhn) — murdered, usually for political reasons

civil war (SIV il wor) — conflict between two or more groups inside the same country

colony (KOL uh nee) — a region ruled by a powerful country, often far away

crusades (kroo SADES) — unsuccessful attempts by Western European Christians to take the Holy Land from the Muslims

democracy (di MOK ruh see) — a form of government where the people elect their own leaders

guerrillas (guh RIL uhs) — small groups that take part in fighting larger forces or armies. They often make surprise raids on an invading enemy.

Holy Land (HOH lee land) — an area of land that is now part of Israel and the Palestinian Territories. It has religious importance to Christians, Jews, and Muslims.

hostages (HOSS tij iz) — people held against their will until certain conditions have been met

Jesuits (JES yoo its) — a Roman Catholic religious order of men

Maronite (ma RUHN ite) — belonging to a Christian group that started in Syria and has close links to the Roman Catholic Church

Middle East (MID uhl eest) — the name of a region that includes many Arab countries like Egypt, Syria, Lebanon, and Iraq, but also Israel, the Palestinian territories, and Iran

militia (muh LISH uh) — an unofficial military group

mines (mines) — a type of bomb that is placed just below the surface of the ground

missionaries (MISH uh ner ees) — religious people who travel abroad to try to convert people in other countries to Christianity

Muslim (MUHZ luhm) — follower of the religion of Islam

National Assembly (NASH uh nuhl uh SEM blee) — the name given to the group of elected representatives of the country

neutral (NOO truhl) — not supporting or helping either side in a conflict or war

refugee (ref yuh JEE) — person who is forced to leave home because of war or other dangerous situation

terrorist (TER ur ist) — person or organization that will use violence to bring about change

United Nations (UN) (yoo NI tid NAY shuhns) — an international organization set up to help promote peace

FURTHER INFORMATION

WEBSITES

CIA Factbook

https://www.cia.gov/library/publications/
the-world-factbook

BBC

http://news.bbc.co.uk/1/hi/world/
middle_east

Lebanese government

www.informs.gov.lb/EN/Main/index.asp

Aljazeera Magazine

www.aljazeera.com

Israeli government

www.gov.il/firstgov/english

Syria Gate

www.syriagate.com

BOOKS

Lebanon: A Question and Answer Book.
Mary Englar. Fact Finders, 2007.

*Lebanon: Enchantment of the World
(Second series).* Terri Willis. Scholastic,
2005.

Lebanon in Pictures. Peter Roop,
Margaret J. Goldstein, and Sam Schultz.
Lerner Publications, 2005.

*Lebanon in the News: Past, Present
And Future.* David Aretha.
Myreportlinks.com 2006.

INDEX